KING ARTHUR

KING ARTHUR

HOWARD PYLE

Retold by
Don Hinkle

Illustrated by
Jerry Tiritilli

Troll Associates

Library of Congress Cataloging in Publication Data

Hinkle, Don.
  King Arthur.

  Summary: Relates how Arthur became a king, married
Guinevere, and suffered his downfall through treachery.
  [1. Arthurian romances. 2. Arthur, King. 3. Knights
and knighthood—Folklore. 4. Folklore—England.]
I. Tiritilli, Jerry, ill. II. Pyle, Howard, 1853-1911.
King Arthur. III. Title.
PZ8.1.H644Ki 1988   398.2´2´´0942   87-15461
ISBN 0-8167-1213-1 (lib. bdg.)
ISBN 0-8167-1214-X (pbk.)

This is the tale of how Arthur became king. In a village churchyard stood a great block of marble, and on it was an iron anvil. Imbedded in the anvil was a magnificent sword. Its blade was made of the finest steel, and its gold hilt was decorated with precious jewels. On the marble block were these words in gold: WHOEVER PULLS FORTH THIS SWORD FROM THE ANVIL IS KING OF ALL ENGLAND.

This was England of long ago, a land of knights and fair ladies, of chivalry and magic. But after the death of King Uther, England became divided, as men fought each other for power. Some fought for land or for a horse. Others fought out of fear or envy. It was a time of constant turmoil. The sound of galloping horses, the clash of sword on armor, and the cries of men in battle echoed throughout the countryside.

Whoever pulls forth this sword from the anvil is king of all England

The citizens of England were tired of the fighting and killing. They wanted a strong king to rule the land again and bring peace. "If we can just find the man who can free the sword from the anvil," the citizens said hopefully, "we shall have a king again."

Many men tried. They sweated and groaned and swore mighty oaths as they tugged at the sword. But it would not budge. The sword remained in the anvil. And England remained without a king.

As the years passed, a series of tournaments were held near the sword in the stone. Tents were set up around a jousting field, and brightly colored flags fluttered in the breeze. The knights were dressed from head to toe in armor. They carried shields and all kinds of weapons: swords, lances, daggers, battle axes, and maces with chains. These knights then jousted on horseback to decide who would try to draw forth the sword.

To one such tournament came Sir Hector with his son Sir Kay and adopted son Arthur, a tall, beardless youth. Sir Kay was strong and bold, charging his horse into the fight. He was determined to win or die trying. Sir Kay fought hard and knocked many men to the ground with his spear and sword. But when he broke his sword on an opponent's shield, he had to stop fighting and leave the field. He shouted to young Arthur, "Quick, brother, bring me a sword from our tent!"

Arthur ran to the family tent, but he could find no swords there. The other men were using them to fight or practice. Knowing his brother needed a sword right away, Arthur looked around the field and saw the sword that was embedded in the anvil. Without thinking, Arthur jumped on top of the stone, grabbed the sword by its hilt, and pulled it out. Then he ran back to Sir Kay.

Sir Kay grabbed the sword from Arthur's hands. He swung it boldly and felt its power. The sword was so strong that it almost flew out of his grip.

"Where did you get this sword?" Sir Kay asked.

"It was stuck in that rock over there," said Arthur. "It didn't seem to belong to anybody, so I took it."

Sir Kay held the sword in front of him, not hearing Arthur's explanation but listening instead to his own thoughts. Surely, Sir Kay thought, this was a sign that I was meant to be king.

He walked about proudly showing the sword. When Sir Hector saw that his son carried the sword from the stone, he gasped, "How did you get this?"

Sir Kay said only, "I broke my own sword and found this instead."

No one had seen Sir Kay take the sword out of the anvil, however. Many knights were doubtful that he had, so a test was ordered. Sir Kay was asked to put the sword back in the anvil and take it out again.

He tried and failed, and tried again and failed again.

At last, young Arthur asked, "May I try?" All the men smiled but they said, "Let him try."

Sir Kay handed the sword to Arthur, who then raised the sword and plunged it into the steel anvil. Then he drew it out again and raised it aloft.

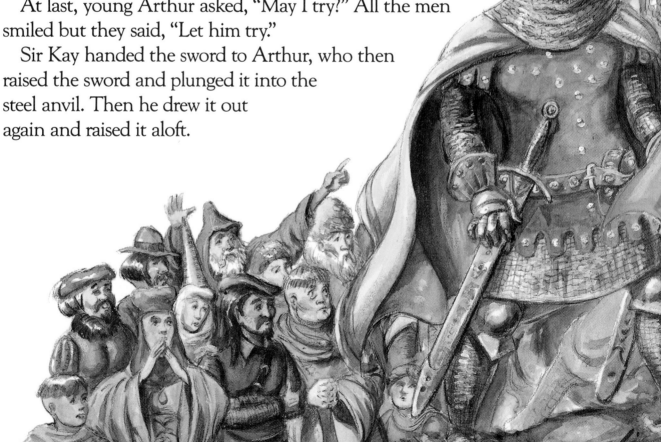

"Does this mean, then, that a beardless boy will be our king?" asked the great warriors. Some said yes, but others said no.

As Arthur withdrew the sword, a tall man in the robes of a wizard stepped forth from the crowd. It was Merlin, the ageless. He said, "This is King Uther's son, Arthur, raised by Sir Hector to protect the boy from Uther's enemies. Now, he's proved by withdrawing the sword that he should rule over all England."

Many brave knights bowed immediately and agreed that Arthur was the rightful king. But others, who were envious and bitter, refused to bow. They said, "It's a plot between Sir Hector and Merlin to plant on the throne a boy of their own choice whose thoughts they can control."

It was not long before this disagreement caused two large opposing armies to be formed. Arthur led his loyal knights into battle like a true king, going into the thick of combat rather than standing protected in the rear. So his knights fought more bravely and easily defeated his enemies.

King Arthur became famous for this victory. Many good men realized that by giving him their allegiance, they could do great deeds for the good of all. And so they came from all parts of the country to King Arthur's castle at Camelot. More noble, honorable knights gathered there than had ever come together before.

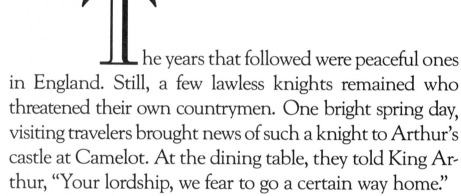

The years that followed were peaceful ones in England. Still, a few lawless knights remained who threatened their own countrymen. One bright spring day, visiting travelers brought news of such a knight to Arthur's castle at Camelot. At the dining table, they told King Arthur, "Your lordship, we fear to go a certain way home."

Arthur asked why, for he thought all roads were safe.

"Because there is a brook that runs too fast for a horse to cross," said the travelers.

"True, but there is a good bridge across that brook," said a knight of the court.

"Yes, but a brutal knight in black armor guards that bridge," they explained. "If anyone tries to cross it, the Black Knight challenges him. No one has succeeded in defeating the Black Knight. He has killed many knights and hung their shields on his tree as a warning to all others."

After King Arthur heard this news, he knew he could not send any knight but himself. So he put on his armor and rode forth on his war-horse to right this wrong.

After he had ridden for a day, King Arthur came upon three evil men with knives pursuing an old man whose beard was white as snow. Arthur leveled his spear, spurred his horse, and thundered toward them. Seeing him, the three thieves dropped their knives and fled.

Turning to the old man, King Arthur then realized he was Merlin. "Ha, Merlin!" laughed Arthur. "With all your magic arts, you would have been killed if I hadn't interfered."

Merlin smiled coldly. "No, I let you save me, for I have come to save you from a far greater peril. I must go with you to meet this Black Knight."

So King Arthur and Merlin rode together through the forest for a long time until they saw a rapid stream rushing through a dark valley. On the far side of a bridge that crossed the stream was a tree hung with many shields. They were stained with blood. Behind the tree was a castle.

Merlin said, "King Arthur, unless you are wise and careful, your shield will hang in that tree."

"That shall be as God wills," said King Arthur. He stepped onto the bridge and saw a shield with these words on it: WHO STRIKES THIS SHIELD DOES SO AT HIS PERIL. He hit the shield and the sound echoed from the walls of the castle. Out of the castle came a huge knight in black armor.

King Arthur said, "I have come, brutal knight, to fight you and to win back all those shields that hang upon your tree."

"You will fail," said the Black Knight, "and your shield will join them."

"The better knight shall win," said King Arthur.

So the two knights rode their horses to opposite sides of a green field. Each raised his shield and lowered his spear, then shouted and spurred his war-horse forward. The two steeds made the ground tremble with their rush, and the two knights hit in the middle of the field with a crash like a thunderbolt. Both spears burst into splinters. The horses staggered back, but neither knight was knocked off his horse. King Arthur was amazed at the strength of his foe.

The Black Knight made a signal and his helper ran from the castle, carrying two more spears. One was handed to each knight. With their fresh spears King Arthur and the Black Knight spurred their horses forward again. Again they clashed. This time, the Black Knight's spear pierced the

shield of King Arthur and knocked him to the ground.
Arthur stood up but staggered dizzily.

"Fight me on foot with your sword!" shouted Arthur.

"No!" replied the Black Knight. "Give me your shield, for
I have unhorsed you."

"I will not!" shouted King Arthur. He grabbed the reins
of the other knight's horse and jerked it so that the Black
Knight fell to the ground.

Both knights drew their swords and rushed together like two wild bulls. They clanged and swung their swords, striking again and again at each other. They knocked whole pieces of armor from each other, baring their flesh and making wounds that stained their armor red.

King Arthur was filled with the madness of battle now. He struck such a monstrous blow with his sword that he broke it. Then the Black Knight raised his sword high and struck King Arthur a blow that sliced through his helmet into his head.

King Arthur's legs buckled and he sank to his knees. Blood and sweat flowed into his eyes inside his helmet. Still, he managed to grab hold of the Black Knight and throw him to the ground. Then King Arthur pulled out a dagger. But he was so weak that the Black Knight took the dagger from his hand.

At that moment, Merlin spoke in a strong voice: "Stop, knight! For he is Arthur, king of all England!"

"I will not stop," cried the Black Knight, set to plunge the dagger into Arthur's chest.

Merlin suddenly raised his staff and struck the Black Knight, who fell to the ground as if he were dead.

King Arthur lifted himself on his elbow and cried out, "Merlin, why have you slain one of the best knights in all the world with your magic?"

"I only put him to sleep, my king," answered Merlin, "but you will soon die unless we heal you."

Merlin put Arthur on his horse and led him to a hut hidden in the forest. A hermit lived there who had great healing powers. And there, as Arthur lay in a fever, his wounds were bathed.

Even with their combined healing arts, Merlin and the hermit were still afraid King Arthur might die of his wounds. His fever grew worse and worse.

One day, the Lady Guinevere came to the forest with her attendants to get a potion from the hermit. Dressed in white robes, she rode on a golden horse. Wherever Lady Guinevere went, she seemed to give off a bright light that penetrated the dark forest.

She entered the hermit's hut and saw King Arthur. Though she did not know who he was, she saw that he was handsome. Arthur, feverish as he was, thought she was a tall slender angel. She gave a box of balsam to the hermit and told him to put it on the knight's wounds. The hermit

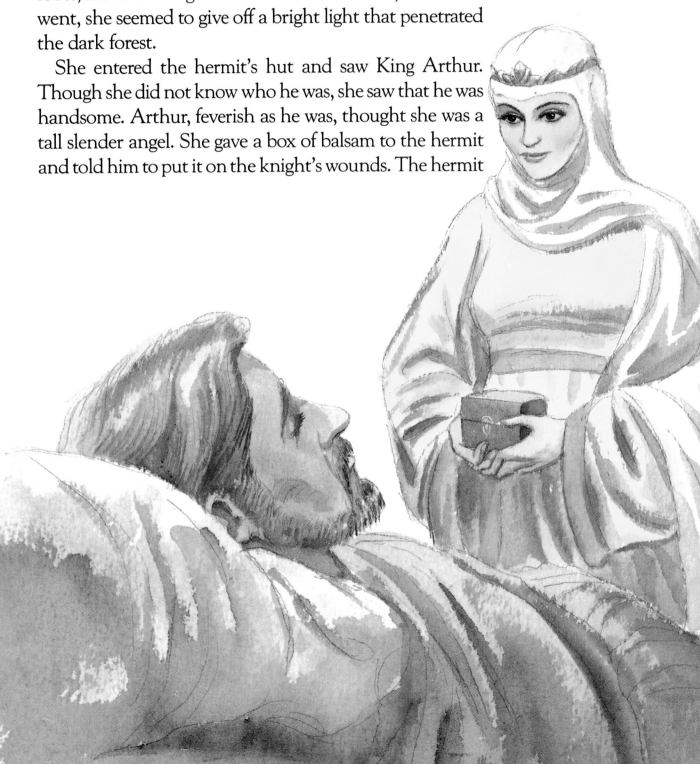

did as he was told and King Arthur immediately fell into a deep, restful sleep. Then the Lady Guinevere departed.

Four days later, King Arthur was completely cured. He walked in the forest, listening to the birds sing, with Merlin beside him.

King Arthur told Merlin that he wanted again to fight the Black Knight who had nearly killed him. Merlin said, "But you have no sword!"

"I shall find a sword," said King Arthur. "But even if I have only a wooden stick, I will fight again with that Black Knight."

"Well," said Merlin, "since you are so determined, perhaps I can help. Not far away is an enchanted lake. In the center of that lake, a woman's arm sometimes appears holding a sword of great beauty. The name of this sword is Excalibur. Many knights have gone to get this sword, but none has ever been able to touch it. Many have died trying. For when any man has approached, either he sinks into the lake or the arm pulls the sword deep into the lake. I will guide you to that lake. Then we will see what happens."

They traveled a great distance. Soon they came to a land where all the air appeared fresh and bright. The trees were in blossom, and their fragrance was sweeter than any King Arthur had ever smelled. In the branches were birds of brilliant colors. The melody of their singing made his heart light. Then he saw the lake, with its bright silver water and flower-covered banks.

Merlin said, "Now that I have brought you here, I can help no more. If you want the sword, you must get it yourself without my help."

In the middle of the lake, King Arthur saw a beautiful arm holding a marvelous sword. He wondered how he might get to it. Then he saw a strange lady walking toward him through the tall grass and flowers. She was dressed in green and wore many jewels and bracelets.

He knew that she was the Lady of the Lake. He kneeled before her.

"Welcome, King Arthur!" she said, gesturing for him to rise.

Arthur then told her about the awful deeds of the Black Knight and said he needed the magical sword in order to fight him.

"The only man who can own this sword," said the Lady of the Lake, "is one who is both fearless and blameless."

"Alas, my lady," said King Arthur, "for though I have as much knightly courage as anyone, I have done some things for which I blame myself. Still, I must try to get Excalibur."

"If you try and you fail, you will die," she said. "But I will help you as much as I can."

The Lady of the Lake softly whistled, and a magic boat moved across the glassy lake. It came toward Arthur and touched the bank. Arthur stepped into the boat and it sped him to the center of the lake where the arm and the sword waited.

King Arthur did not hesitate. He reached out for the sword. Immediately the arm disappeared beneath the water, leaving the sword and its scabbard in his hand. Arthur's heart swelled with joy, for Excalibur was a hundred times more beautiful than even the sword in the anvil.

With Excalibur sheathed at his side, King Arthur returned to the valley of the Black Knight and challenged him to combat again.

The fighting was more ferocious than the first time. Both knights were knocked from their horses. But they staggered to their feet, pulled out their swords, and fought.

With the magic of Excalibur, King Arthur soon overcame his enemy, giving him several wounds without being wounded himself. Then King Arthur struck the Black Knight so hard that he fell to his knees.

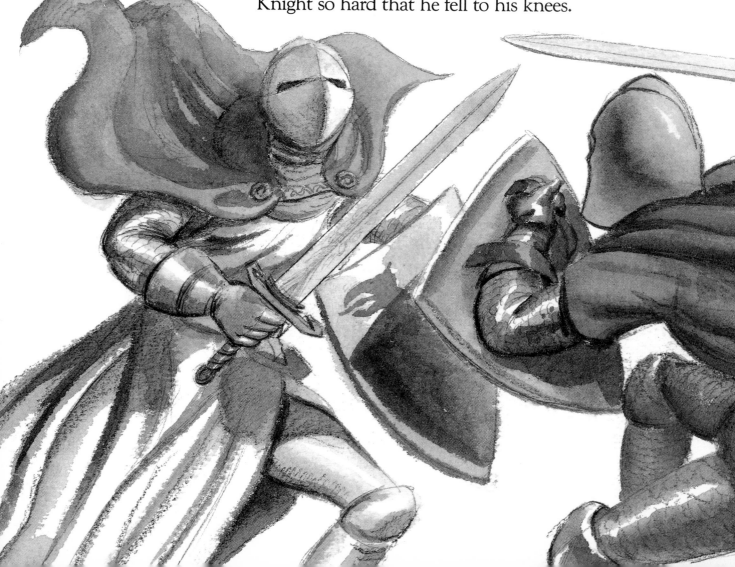

The Black Knight said, "Kill me if you wish. But if you are king, show me mercy. Spare my life, and I swear that I will serve you with all my heart and soul."

"You are one of the best fighters I have ever met," said King Arthur. "I forgive you." And so King Arthur turned a bitter enemy into a friend and gained his loyalty.

Then King Arthur and Merlin rode off through the forest back toward Camelot. Arthur's heart sang, and sunlight shone on his armor as if he were covered in glory.

Merlin asked, "If you had to make a choice, which would you keep—Excalibur or the sheath that holds it?"

"Ha! I'd much rather have Excalibur!"

"Poor choice," replied Merlin. "Although Excalibur is so great a sword that it can cut in two a feather or a bar of iron, the sheath will protect you from wounds or even from losing a single drop of blood."

King Arthur grew sad. "Then I haven't done anything by myself," he said glumly. "What good is a knight who needs magic to defeat his enemy? I will return this sword and sheath to the Lady of the Lake."

Merlin said, "My king, remember that you are no ordinary knight but a king. Your life belongs not to you but to all the people you protect. They cannot fight or defend themselves from evildoers."

King Arthur thought for a long time before he spoke. Then he said, "For the sake of my people, I will keep Excalibur to fight for them and the sheath to preserve my life. But I will use this sword only in time of great danger."

Arthur decided that when he returned to the castle at Camelot, he would build a strongbox to hold Excalibur. He would remove it only when it was needed to protect the kingdom.

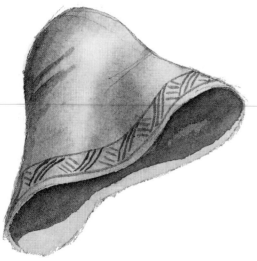

During this same ride back to Camelot, Arthur told Merlin that he had fallen in love with a tall and beautiful lady in the hermit's hut.

"Ah," Merlin said, "that is the Lady Guinevere, daughter of a nobleman who lives in a nearby castle."

"I wish I could know her better," said Arthur. "Perhaps she might also fall in love with me."

Merlin smiled. "You have merely to ask her, and she would gladly be your wife."

"But only because I am king," cried Arthur. "I want her to love me for myself."

"That may not be possible," said Merlin doubtfully.

"But you say all things are possible to those who have pure hearts and minds," argued King Arthur.

"Perhaps there is a way," Merlin said. "I will think about it." After a while, Merlin pulled a cap from his pocket and handed it to Arthur.

"What do you want me to do with this?" Arthur said.

"Put it on," said Merlin.

"This is a peasant's cap," laughed Arthur.

After they had ridden for a while longer, Arthur asked, "Why do you want me to remove my knight's helmet and wear a simple cap?"

"To stop you from asking so many questions," Merlin said gruffly.

Quietly, Arthur removed his helmet and put the cap on. As he did, he felt a change in himself. When he came upon a small lake and guided his horse to the edge of the water, Arthur looked at his reflection in it. He saw a humble, beardless peasant staring back at him—not a noble king at all!

"What have you done to me!" he cried.

Merlin turned and saw that Arthur was now wearing the cap. He said, "With that disguise, you can visit the Lady Guinevere as you wish."

"Then I'll part with you here and ride to her castle at once," said Arthur.

"One warning, my king," said the wizard. "You may find it harder to be a peasant than to be a king and knight."

"Nonsense!" declared Arthur. "For me this will be a holiday, and I'll be near the one I adore."

So, wearing the cap, King Arthur entered the castle of Lady Guinevere's father.

"What do you want here, fellow?" asked the guard at the gate.

"Merely to work for his lordship," said Arthur.

"Go to the back of the garden. You'll find the gardener's cottage there. See if they can use some help."

Luckily help was needed, and Arthur was employed as a gardener. And each day as Lady Guinevere walked among the flowers and trees, the humble peasant watched her and admired her even more.

Lady Guinevere soon sensed that there was more to this gardener than met the eye. One day, she asked him to bring a bouquet of roses to her rooms.

"Gladly, my lady," Arthur said, bowing. He went to the rose garden and picked a bouquet of the finest flowers, both small buds and large blooms, colored red and pink and yellow.

When he had an armful, Arthur appeared in her room, bearing the roses. "Take off your cap in the presence of the daughter of a great lord!" cried the ladies in waiting.

26

King Arthur said, "Lady, I cannot take off my cap."
"And why not?" asked Guinevere.

Thinking quickly, Arthur replied. "It hides an ugly place upon my head."

"Oh, then," she laughed, "keep it on your head by all means. But bring me the roses."

He approached where she sat and kneeled before her, extending his hand with the roses. With these, dear lady, I pledge my heart to you, he thought.

Lady Guinevere quickly snatched the cap from his head, and he was instantly transformed. Instead of a humble gardener, there stood a noble young knight.

Guinevere now recognized him as the knight who lay sorely wounded in the hermit's hut in the forest. But since she knew he was no danger to her, she pretended not to recognize him. Guinevere laughed and flung back his cap.

Arthur put on his cap and returned to the garden. He was more in love with her than ever.

Soon afterward, a grim-looking, angry knight dressed in gray appeared outside the walls of the castle. He marched his horse back and forth, and shouted a challenge to Guinevere's father.

"Fight me in battle or grant me my requests," called the Gray Knight. He not only wanted to marry the beautiful Guinevere, but also to be given some of the lands owned by her father. Her father refused to grant these requests, but none of his knights would come forth to fight the villain.

As Arthur snipped twigs in the garden and heard the bully shouting outside the wall, he decided that he would have to take action against him.

Next day, the Gray Knight again paraded on his gray horse outside the gate of the castle. But within the castle grounds, a knight in white armor, mounted on a white horse, appeared beneath the window of Lady Guinevere.

She gazed down at him and asked, "Strange knight, will you be my father's champion in battle against this bold ruffian?"

"Whatever you may wish to have done, I shall do, fair maiden," King Arthur declared. "But I ask for a token from you to wear as I fight him."

"You have it," she said. She removed from her neck a pearl necklace and dropped it down to him. He caught it on his lance and wrapped it around his sleeve. Then the white-armored champion spurred his horse toward the gate. When he came through it, his armor flared in the bright sunlight.

The Gray Knight came near and spoke to him. "I see that you wear no crest on your helmet or on your shield, so I know not who you are. You could be an ordinary peasant pretending to be a knight. But I suspect you are a knight of noble bearing and proven courage, or you would not have dared come out to fight me."

"That is so, Sir Knight," said King Arthur. "I am of a quality equal to yours. As for my courage, it has been proved in as many fights as has yours."

"Sir Stranger," said the Gray Knight, "you speak like one with a bold spirit. But say your prayers, for I shall cast you down with such force that you will never rise again. I have done that to better men than you."

To this King Arthur answered calmly, "That shall be according to the will of heaven, Sir Knight, and not according to your will."

The knights saluted each other and rode to opposite sides of the field. Each then lowered his spear and raised his shield to make ready. A silence fell upon all the onlookers. For a

moment, each knight sat like a statue made of iron. Then—suddenly—each shouted to his war-horse and launched forth. They met in the midst of the field with a noise like a violent thunderclap.

The spear of the Gray Knight broke but King Arthur's did not. The Gray Knight was knocked backward out of his saddle. He whirled in the air like a windmill and hit the ground so hard that it shuddered. All the onlookers shouted their happiness. They knew the Gray Knight would never rise again. He lay dead where he had fallen.

The next morning, Lady Guinevere's father spoke with her. He said, "My daughter, you are old enough to consider marrying a man who will cherish and protect you from your enemies. This champion in white armor who has slain the Gray Knight could be your own champion and husband. I think it would be well if you turn your heart to him as he has appeared to turn his heart to you."

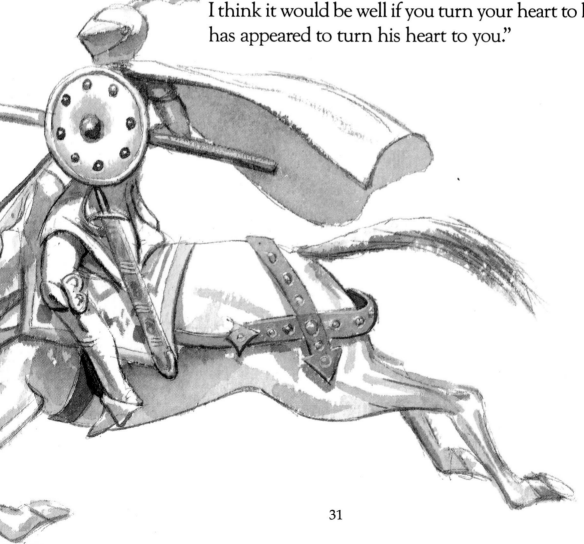

At these words, Lady Guinevere said, "My lord and father, if I give my heart as wife to anyone, I will give it only to the gardener who digs in my garden."

"Do you mock me?" her father asked in anger.

"Never, my lord! I tell you truly, this same gardener knows more about the champion knight than anyone else."

The gardener was summoned by a messenger to appear in the presence of her father. When he stood there with his head bowed but cap on, her father spoke angrily, saying, "Do you not have the grace to remove your hat in my presence?"

"I cannot, my lord," replied the gardener.

Lady Guinevere's father grabbed his sword, thinking to remove both cap and head. But Lady Guinevere spoke quietly. "Please remove your cap in my father's presence."

"As you wish, my lady." The gardener removed his cap. But he was a gardener no more.

Guinevere's father cried, "My lord and my king!" He knelt upon the floor before King Arthur.

Lady Guinevere was also astonished. She trembled now, for she realized that she had mocked and jested with the king. She put her hand to her heart and went to the window.

King Arthur walked over to her. He took her hand and said, "Lady, are you well?"

"Lord, I fear your greatness," she replied.

"No, my lady!" he said. "Rather, I am afraid of you. For your kind regard is dearer to me than anything else in the world. Otherwise, I would not have worked as a gardener in your garden, hoping to earn your good favor."

"You have my good favor," said Guinevere.

"Have I your good will in great measure?" he asked.

"Yes, you have it in very great measure."

Then Arthur bent his head and kissed her before all who were there, and he pledged their marriage. Her father was filled with joy. He wanted to give a great, precious gift to accompany his daughter in marriage to the king. But he couldn't think of any gift that seemed adequate. When Merlin later visited to attend the great feast in honor of Arthur and Guinevere's marriage, the father asked Merlin for his thoughts on a gift.

Merlin said, "Long ago I gave King Uther a round table of oak. It could seat fifty men who were the worthiest knights in England. The knights' names were written in gold letters on the table. Now, the table sits empty in a room of your castle, waiting for new and splendid knights to surround it with glory once again."

"This is true," agreed the lord. "But what shall I do?"

"If you give that table to the son of King Uther, King Arthur," answered Merlin, "I guarantee it will once again resound with tales of great deeds and daring."

"Indeed," said Guinevere's father, "a perfect gift for a perfect king like Arthur!"

The official proclamation of Lady Guinevere and King Arthur's upcoming marriage delighted the people of England. Arthur had by then returned to Camelot, while Guinevere had stayed behind to prepare for her journey.

Now ready and wearing a gown that only heightened her beauty, she set out with her finely dressed lady attendants on the road to Camelot. Handsome knights rode beside them. Jesters and clowns joked and laughed, and jugglers and minstrels performed. Behind them all was a special wagon carrying the immense Round Table.

When Guinevere arrived at Camelot, she looked up and saw King Arthur standing on a castle tower, watching her. He came down to greet her. She turned and bowed low before him, and held out her hands to offer him a bouquet of fine roses.

They were married within the week, and all of England celebrated their royal wedding.

35

After the wedding, Arthur and Merlin began choosing the knights who would sit at the Round Table. As each knight was selected, his name would appear in gold on the table where he'd be sitting. Once all the knights were chosen, they swore to this covenant of the Knighthood of the Round Table: "I will be gentle to the weak. I will be courageous to the strong. I will be terrible to the wicked and the evildoer. I will defend the helpless who call upon me for aid. I will defend my fellow knights of the Round Table. I will be merciful to all good folk and be gentle in deeds, true in friendships, and faithful in love."

This was their covenant, and each knight swore it upon the cross of his sword, kissing the hilt to seal the bond.

As Merlin had prophesied, the Round Table was again filled with brave knights. And it remained so until those years of glory, chivalry, and knighthood ended.

The next few years were peaceful ones in England. But trouble was brewing within Arthur's own family. Morgana La Fey, Arthur's half-sister, hated him. She imagined that he had insulted her in various ways. And so with her son, Sir Mordred, Morgana began plotting against the king.

First, she wove a magic web of deceit and trapped Merlin in it. Merlin was no longer able to protect Arthur. Then, having learned the secret of Excalibur and its sheath, Morgana decided to rob King Arthur of one or both.

Her opportunity came during a visit to Camelot. She kept talking about the sword until Arthur finally showed it to her. She admired it greatly, saying how beautiful it was and how lovely it would look hanging on a wall in her castle. In front of a number of noble knights and ladies, Morgana asked King Arthur to let her keep it for a time. "Whenever you need Excalibur, I'll send it to you through the magic that Merlin taught me before he disappeared," she lied.

Arthur was unaware of Morgana's hatred for him. And since there was no war and no enemies he knew about, Arthur thought that his kingdom was not in peril. So Arthur agreed to let Morgana borrow Excalibur, hoping to please her.

Back in her own castle, Morgana asked some craftsmen skilled in gold and metal to make an imitation sword and scabbard. Once they finished, no one could tell Excalibur from its counterfeit. Morgana then returned the false sword and sheath to King Arthur, who immediately locked them in his strongbox.

Next, she used her wizardly arts to entice a bold and brave knight to fight for her. She gave him the real Excalibur and its real sheath, but did not tell him this. Then she cast a spell on him, confusing his mind so much that he could no longer recognize King Arthur.

In the meantime, she had also convinced King Arthur that her knight was a dangerous threat to his kingdom. Arthur believed he could not win a battle against this knight without using Excalibur, so he opened his strongbox and removed the false sword and sheath.

Morgana watched from a distance as King Arthur went into battle with what he thought was the real Excalibur. But no matter how hard Arthur struck with his sword, he could not cut the armor of the other knight. Arthur was baffled, for Excalibur had never failed him before. He was also seriously wounded, bleeding heavily, while his opponent showed not even a scratch.

Has Excalibur lost its strength? he silently asked himself.

Arthur struck again with what he supposed was the magic sword, and yet he still could not penetrate his enemy's armor. Finally, his sword broke, and the brave knight who fought against him said, "I cannot kill you while you are weaponless, so you must surrender."

"That I can never do," King Arthur replied, picking up the broken sword near his feet.

The other knight raised his sword to strike a fatal blow. But as he did so, Arthur recognized the sword as the true Excalibur.

"You have my sword, Excalibur!" he exclaimed.

This so surprised the other knight that Arthur was able to take the sword from him and win the battle.

However, Arthur was so badly wounded and bleeding that he had to be put to bed in his tent to recover. An angry Morgana La Fey crept into his tent. She could not steal Excalibur because Arthur gripped it while he slept. But she found the sheath and hid it under her cape.

As she left the tent, a guard spoke to her: "How is your brother, the king, my lady?"

"He seems to be resting well," she said, keeping the sheath concealed. "I'm sure he will be better soon." Morgana wasted no time in mounting her horse and fleeing quickly with the sheath.

When Arthur awoke and realized that Excalibur's sheath was gone, he leaped from his bed and ran outside. "Who has been in my tent?" he asked of the guard standing close by.

"Only your sister, Morgana La Fey," the guard replied.

King Arthur quickly mounted a horse and took off in pursuit. Morgana La Fey, however, looked behind her from a high hill and saw Arthur following her. She swore that he would not regain the sheath.

For days, Morgana rode as fast as she could until she reached a lake and threw the sheath into it. As she did so, a beautiful arm reached out of the water, grabbed the sheath, waved it back and forth twice, then sank beneath the surface.

Morgana's son, Sir Mordred was working evil against the king in another way. Sir Mordred spread vicious gossip in the court about the love between Queen Guinevere and one of the Round Table's bravest knights, Sir Lancelot. It was true they loved each other, but not in the way Mordred had described. Nevertheless, some people at the court started believing Mordred's lies.

When Arthur returned to Camelot without the sheath or his wicked half-sister, he was told of the ugly rumor about Guinevere and Sir Lancelot. Arthur was stunned by what seemed to be treachery under his own roof. With great sorrow, he banished Sir Lancelot from his court and from England, sending him far across the sea.

Afterward, Sir Mordred started spreading more malicious lies. He said that Sir Lancelot was assembling a mighty army across the sea so that he could return and take away the kingdom from King Arthur. Further confused by these lies, King Arthur soon made war against Sir Lancelot. He set out after Lancelot in ships with many soldiers. But before he left, Arthur asked Sir Mordred to rule in his absence in order to protect the kingdom.

While Arthur warred against Lancelot's army, Sir Mordred and Morgana La Fey continued to plot against him. They sent messengers to Camelot, bearing a false message that said King Arthur had been killed in the war.

Mother and son then managed to have Mordred chosen king. After Mordred was crowned, he announced that he would marry Guinevere. He thought that would make the people love him and forget Arthur. Queen Guinevere, however, refused. She escaped to a high tower and was protected there by some knights still loyal to Arthur, even though they thought he was dead.

While Arthur was fighting on a foreign shore, he heard news about Mordred's capture of his kingdom. Immediately, Arthur pulled his army out of battle and sailed for England. As his ship approached the English coast, Arthur could see Mordred and his mighty army waiting on the shore.

"He is ready to ruin the kingdom in a ruthless war," Arthur

muttered. His knights advised him to meet with Mordred under a flag of truce.

King Arthur agreed, though he warned his army that if they saw any sword drawn, they were to fight fiercely and kill the traitor Mordred.

During the truce meeting, King Arthur said, "Let us have peace now in the kingdom while I live. After I die, Mordred may rule. I hope he rules well and for the good of all." It seemed as if an agreement would be reached.

But Morgana would not be denied. She hated Arthur so much that she used her witchcraft once more to try to destroy him. Morgana cast a spell on a snake, which then bit the foot of a knight in Sir Mordred's army. The knight quickly drew his sword and cut the snake in half. But the flash of the blade was seen by all the soldiers. Instantly the two armies clashed in battle.

43

The fighting raged until all were dead but King Arthur and one of his knights. The knight said, "Look, my king! Sir Mordred rests on his sword over there. Make peace with him."

But King Arthur said, "He shall never escape my hands." Then, taking his spear in his hands, Arthur ran toward Sir Mordred and shouted, "Traitor! Now you die!"

Hearing this, Sir Mordred drew his sword and ran at King Arthur. When the two collided, King Arthur thrust Mordred through the body with his spear, killing him. But before Mordred died, his sword pierced the helmet of King Arthur, who fell to the ground.

King Arthur knew he was fatally wounded. He told his knight to take Excalibur and throw it in the nearest lake.

The knight did as commanded. And as he hurled it, a beautiful arm and hand rose from the water, caught the spinning sword, shook it twice, and then vanished beneath the water.

Returning, the knight helped the wounded King Arthur to the sea. There, bathed in a mystical light, a ship waited for him. It had no crew or captain.

"Put me on that ship," King Arthur commanded. The knight helped Arthur to the ship, then let the king board by himself. As soon as Arthur was on deck, the ship turned and sailed away toward the setting sun.

What happened to King Arthur after that is not known. Some people say that King Arthur died and was buried in a chapel. But many say that King Arthur never died at all. They say he only rests, and that someday he will reclaim Excalibur and its sheath and rule again over England. For on his tomb is written this verse: HERE LIES ARTHUR, KING THAT WAS, AND KING THAT SHALL BE.

Here Lies Arthur,

King That Was,

And King That Shall Be.